The Perfect Cat Anthology

Jill and Martin Leman

PELHAM BOOKS

First published in Great Britain in 1983 by
Pelham Books Ltd, 44 Bedford Square, London WC1B 3DU
Reprinted 1984

ISBN 0 7207 1472 9

Printed and bound in Italy by New Interlitho

A house without a cat, and a well-fed well-petted,
and properly revered cat, may be a perfect house,
perhaps, but how can it prove its title?!

Mark Twain

Miss Tibbles is my kitten; white
as day she is and black as night.

She moves in little gusts and breezes
sharp and sudden as a sneeze is.

At hunting Tibbles has no match.
How I like to see her catch

moth or beetle, two a penny,
and feast until there isn't any!

or, if they 'scape her, see her eyes
grow big as saucers with surprise.

Sometimes I like her calm, unwild,
 gentle as a sleeping child,

and wonder as she lies, a fur ring,
curled upon my lap, unstirring, –
is it me or Tibbles purring?

Ian Serraillier · Miss Tibbles

NAT'S CATS

Over the hearth with my 'minishing eyes I muse
Until after
The last coal dies.
Every tunnel of the mouse,
Every channel of the cricket,
I have smelt.
I have felt
The secret shifting of the mouldered rafter,
And heard
Every bird in the thicket.
I see
You
Nightingale up in your tree!
I, born of a race of strange things,
Of deserts, great temples, great kings,
In the hot sands where the nightingale never sings!

Ford Madox Ford · The cat of the house

FRED

Three tabbies took out their cats to tea,
As well-behaved tabbies as well could be:
Each sat in the chair that each preferred,
They mewed for their milk, and they sipped and purred.
Now tell me this (as these cats you've seen them) –
How many lives had these cats between them?

Kate Greenaway · Three Tabbies

JANET'S CATS

My old cat stretches out his arm,
To say, 'I and You.'
He thinks the future threatens harm;
I feel it too.
The flexing paw to reassure
Myself and creature
Asserts, in feline comfiture,
Our frail, shared nature.

Robert Gittings · Cat

GINGER

Hark! She is calling to her cat.
She is down the misty garden in a tatter-brim straw hat,
And broken slippers grass-wet, treading tearful daisies.
But he does not heed her. He sits still – and gazes.

Where the laden gooseberry leans over to the rose,
He sits, thorn-protected, gazing down his nose.
Coffee-coloured skies above him press upon the sun;
Bats about his mistress flitter-flutter one by one;

Jessamines drop perfume; the nightingales begin;
Nightjars wind their humdrum notes; a crescent moon rides thin;
The daybird chorus dies away, the air shrinks chill and grey.
Her lonely voice still calls him – but her panther won't come in!

Richard Church · The Cat

BEN

The Girls wake, stretch, and pad up to the door.
    They rub my leg and purr:
    One sniffs around my shoe,
    Rich with an outside smell,
  The other rolls back on the floor –
White bib exposed, and stomach of soft fur.

Now, more awake, they re-enact Ben Hur
    Along the corridor,
    Wheel, gallop; as they do,
    Their noses twitching still,
  Their eyes get wild, their bodies tense,
Their usual prudence seemingly withdraws.

And then they wrestle: parry, lock of paws,
    Blind hug of close defence,
    Tail-thump, and smothered mew.
    If either, though, feel claws,
  She abruptly rises, knowing well
How to stalk off in wise indifference.

Thom Gunn · Apartment cats

PIP AND SQUEAK

Now Tom's translated, not a mouse
Dare inhabit Heaven's house;
Cherubim shall bring him milk,
Seraphs stroke his coat of silk
While, with whiskers aureoled,
He shall walk the streets of gold
Or, happily relaxed, lie prone,
Deeply purring, by the throne.

Vivien Bulkley · Cat of cats

PHARAOH

He blinks upon the hearth-rug
And yawns in deep content,
Accepting all the comforts
That Providence has sent.

Louder he purrs, and louder,
In one glad hymn of praise,
For all the nights' adventures,
For quiet, restful days.

Life will go on for ever,
With all that cat can wish;
Warmth, and the glad procession
Of fish, and milk and fish.

Only – the thought disturbs him –
He's noticed once or twice,
The times are somehow breeding
A nimbler race of mice.

Alexander Gray · On a cat ageing

PRUDENCE

Cat, if you go outdoors, you must walk in the snow.
You will come back with little white shoes on your feet,
little white shoes of snow that have heels of sleet.
Stay by the fire, my Cat. Lie still, do not go.
See how the flames are leaping and hissing low,
I will bring you a saucer of milk like a marguerite,
so white and so smooth, so spherical and so sweet –
stay with me, Cat. Outdoors the wild winds blow.

Outdoors the wild winds blow, Mistress, and dark is the night,
strange voices cry in the trees, intoning strange lore,
and more than cats move, lit by our eyes' green light,
on silent feet where the meadow grasses hang hoar –
Mistress, there are portents abroad of magic and might,
and things that are yet to be done. Open the door!

Elizabeth Coatsworth · On a night of snow

SANDY

She moved through the garden in glory, because
She had very long claws at the end of her paws.
Her back was arched, her tail was high,
A green fire glared in her vivid eye;
And all the Toms, though never so bold,
Quailed at the martial Marigold.

Richard Garnett · Marigold

THE BONIS HALL CATS

The tortoiseshell cat
She sits on the mat
As gay as a sunflower she;
In orange and black you see her blink,
And her waistcoat's white, and her nose is pink,
And her eyes are green of the sea.
But all is vanity, all the way;
Twilight's coming, and close of day,
And every cat in the twilight's grey,
Every possible cat.

The tortoiseshell cat,
She is smooth and fat,
And we call her Josephine,
Because she weareth upon her back
This coat of colours, this raven black,
This red of the tangerine.
But all is vanity, all the way;
Twilight follows the brightest day,
And every cat in the twilight's grey,
Every possible cat.

Patrick R. Chalmers · The tortoiseshell cat

SCRUFFTY AND LILY

Come here little Puss
And I'll make you quite smart,
You shall wear this gold chain,
And I'll wear this fine heart:
And when we are drest,
My dear Aunty shall see
Who then will look best,
Little Pussy or me!

Anon · Fanny and her cat

BETTY

Half loving-kindliness, and half disdain,
Thou comest to my call serenely suave,
With humming speech and gracious gestures grave,
In salutation courtly and urbane:
Yet must I humble me thy grace to gain –
For wiles may win thee, but no arts enslave,
And nowhere gladly thou abidest save
Where naught disturbs the concord of thy reign.
Sphinx of my quiet hearth! who deignst to dwell,
Friend of my toil, companion of mine ease,
Thine is the lore of Rā and Rameses;
That men forget dost thou remember well,
Beholden still in blinking reveries,
With sombre sea-green eyes inscrutable.

Rosamund Marriott Watson · To my cat

COASTGUARD'S CAT

I wish she wouldn't ask me if
I love the kitten more than her.
Of course I love her –
But I love the kitten too,
And it has fur...

Anon

FLUFFY

I like black cats because:

They are discreetly dressed for every occasion

They bring good luck to their owners

If wearing a white bow-tie they make excellent butlers

They are dramatic by day and invisible by night

They make unwelcome visitors feel ill at ease by suddenly looking sinister

The black leather on their paws and nose is always in good taste
and very durable

They enjoy Hallowe'en parties

Their pleasing sobriety of manner fits them for unobtrusive duties
in undertakers' parlours, public libraries, ladies' waiting rooms
and the better kind of family restaurant

When they stretch their fore-paws they appear to be wearing
long black elbow-length evening gloves

They are used to riding pillion when I fly across the sky at night

Anon

BUSTER

Here's my baby's bread and milk,
For her lip, as soft as silk;
Here's the basin, clean and neat;
Here's the spoon of silver sweet;
Here's the stool, and here's the chair,
For my little lady fair.

No, you must not spill it out,
And drop the bread and milk about;
But let it stand before you flat,
And pray, remember pussy cat:
Poor old pussy cat, that purrs
All so patiently for hers.

True, she runs about the house,
Catching, now and then, a mouse,
But, though she thinks it very nice,
That only makes a tiny slice;
So don't forget, that you should stop,
And leave poor puss a little drop.

Anon · Breakfast and puss

SMUDGE AND SPIKE

C'est un grand *Monsieur* Pussy-Cat
Who lives on the mat
Devant un feu énorme
And that is why he is so fat,
En effet il sait quelque chose
Et fait chanter son hôte,
Raison de plus pourquoi
He has such a glossy coat.
Ah ha, Monsieur Pussy-Cat,
Si grand et si gras,
Take care you don't *pousser trop*
The one who gives you such *jolis plats.*

Stevie Smith · Monsieur Pussy-Cat, Blackmailer

CAROLINE'S CAT

O little cat with yellow eyes,
Enthroned upon my garden gate,
Remote, impassive and sedate
And so unutterably wise.

You seem to watch a world that lies
Behind us – where the shadows wait,
O little cat with yellow eyes,
Enthroned upon my garden gate!

Where visions of the past arise,
Of honoured dust and royal state,
And Pharaohs bowed to call you great.

Or are you merely spotting flies,
O little cat with yellow eyes?

Helen Vaughan Williams · O little cat with yellow eyes

LUCY

Cats sleep
Anywhere,
Any table,
Any chair,
Top of piano,
Window-ledge,
In the middle,
On the edge,
Open drawer,
Empty shoe,
Anybody's
Lap will do,
Fitted in a
Cardboard box,
In the cupboard
With your frocks –
Anywhere!
They don't care!
Cats sleep
Anywhere.

Eleanor Farjeon · Cats

TIGGER AND SMUDGE

As I was going to St Ives
I met a man with seven wives,
Each wife had seven sacks,
Each sack had seven cats,
Each cat had seven kits,
Kits, cats, sacks and wives,
How many were going to St Ives?

Answer: only one

SMEATON'S PIER

Unfussy lodger, she knows what she wants and gets it:
Food, cushions, fires, the run of the garden.
I, her night porter in the small hours,
Don't bother to grumble, grimly let her in.
To that coldness she purrs assent,
Eats her fill and outwits me,
Plays hide and seek in the dark house.

Only at times, by chance meeting the gaze
Of her amber eyes that can rest on me
As on a beech-bole, on bracken or meadow grass
I'm moved to celebrate the years between us,
The farness and the nearness:
My fingers graze her head.
To that fondness she purrs assent.

Michael Hamburger · Cat

JUMPERS

O lovely bit
Of silky fur
Jewel-eyed
Aristocrat
I'd wear you
To the Opera
If you were
Not my cat.

Muriel Schulz · Aristocrat

R E D

As Pussy sat upon the step,
Taking the nice fresh air,
A neighbour's little dog came by,
Ah, Pussy are you there?
Good morning, Mistress Pussy Cat,
Come, tell me how do you do?
Quite well, I thank you, Puss replied:
Now tell me how are you?

Anon · Little puss

SCRUFFTY

Two cats
One up a tree
One under the tree
The cat up a tree is he
The cat under the tree is she
The tree is wych elm, just incidentally.
He takes no notice of she, she takes no notice of he.
He stares at the woolly clouds passing, she stares at the tree.
There's been a lot written about cats, by Old Possum, Yeats, and Company,
But not Alfred de Musset or Lord Tennyson or Poe or anybody
Wrote about one cat under, and one cat up, a tree.
God knows why this should be left to me
Except I like cats as cats be
Especially one cat up
And one cat under
A wych elm
Tree.

Ewart Milne · Diamond cut diamond

TIBBY AND SCAMPER

Sometimes I am an unseen
marmalade cat, the friendliest colour,
making off through a window without permission,
pacing along a broken-glass wall to the greenhouse,
jumping down with a soft, four-pawed thump,
finding two inches open of the creaking door
with the !oose brass handle,
slipping impossibly in,
flattening my fur at the hush and touch of the sudden warm air,
avoiding the tiled gutter of slow green water,
skirting the potted nests of tetchy cactuses,
and sitting with my tail flicked
skilfully underneath me, to sniff
the azaleas the azaleas   the azaleas.

Alan Brownjohn · Cat

SUNNY

Martin Leman would like to thank the following people who either
commissioned or allowed him to paint their cats:
Natalie Gibson, NAT'S CATS and JUMPERS; Adrianne LeMan, FRED and GINGER;
Janet Foreman, JANET'S CATS; John and Lesley Lear, BEN;
Mr and Mrs TM Flynn, PRUDENCE; Royd's Advertising, THE BONIS HALL CATS;
Ron, Chrissie and James Bridle, BUSTER; Eve Catlett, SPIKE and SMUDGE;
Caroline Oakes, CAROLINE'S CAT; John and Eileen Killingley, RED;
Belinda Blackburn, TIGGER and SMUDGE;
Sarah and Paul Hellings Wheeler, TIBBY and SCAMPER.

For permission to use poems we should like to thank: Ian Serraillier for 'Miss Tibbles' ©
1950; David Higham Associates Ltd for 'The Cat of the House' by Ford Madox Ford;
Heinemann Educational Books Ltd for 'Cat' by Robert Gittings from *Collected Poems*;
Laurence Pollinger Ltd and the Estate of Richard Church for 'The Cat' by Richard Church
from *Collected Poems*; Harrap & Co Ltd for 'Cat of Cats' by Vivien Bulkley and 'On a cat
ageing' by Alexander Gray, from *The Poet's Cat* edited by Mona Gooden; Faber & Faber Ltd
and Farrar, Straus & Giroux Inc for 'Apartment Cats' by Thom Gunn from *Moly*; Mark
Paterson on behalf of Elizabeth Coatsworth for 'On a night of snow'; Methuen, London for
'The Tortoiseshell Cat' by Patrick R Chalmers from *A Peck o' Maut*; James MacGibbon, the
Executor of the Estate of Stevie Smith, for 'Monsieur Pussy-cat, Blackmailer' from *The
Collected Poems of Stevie Smith*; Rosalie Mander, editor of *CAT-egories*, published by
Weidenfeld and Nicholson Ltd for 'O little cat with yellow eyes' by Helen Vaughan Williams;
Oxford University Press Ltd and Harold Ober Associates for 'Cats' by Eleanor Farjeon from
The Children's Bells; Michael Hamburger for 'Cat' from *Travelling* published by the Fulcrum
Press; Ewart Milne and The Bodley Head Ltd for 'Diamond cut diamond'; Macmillan,
London and Basingstoke for 'Cat' by Alan Brownjohn from *Brownjohn's Beasts*.
Every effort has been made to trace the copyright owners of the material used in this
anthology. The editor and publishers apologise for any omissions, and would be pleased to
hear from those whom they were unable to trace.

PELHAM BOOKS